Disney's Winnie the Pooh

Annual 2001

Editor / Designer: Lisa Carless
© Disney. Based on the Pooh stories by A.A. Milne. © The Pooh Properties Trust.
Published in Great Britain in 2000 by Egmont World Ltd, a division of Egmont Holding Ltd,
Deanway Technology Centre, Wilmslow Road, Handforth, Cheshire SK9 3FB.
Printed in Italy. ISBN 0-7498-4865-0.

£5.99
UK only

D0549056

Hello, boys and girls!

Welcome to the Hundred Acre Wood with Winnie the Pooh and all his friends. Why don't you join in the fun and games?

We've hidden lots of little objects throughout your annual - see how many you find of each one and write that number in the box next to it. Have fun finding them!

Contents

The falling star

1 Pooh and his friends had been playing Cowboys and Indians all day. They were having so much fun they didn't realise it was getting late.

"Look, it's almost dark," said Sheriff Christopher Robin, "I think we'd better finish the game." So they all waved goodbye and set off home.

3 Piglet was spending the night at Pooh's house, so they walked home together. "What a starry night," said Piglet, looking up at the sky.

4 Piglet gazed at all the stars twinkling in the sky. Then he gasped. "Look at that star - it's falling!" he told Pooh.

5 The star was falling towards the ground. "Let's try and catch it!" said Pooh. They ran after the star but it fell down behind a bush

6 "Oh dear, the poor star. We must find it," said Piglet, looking in the leaves. "It's got to be here somewhere," Pooh said, searching the ground.

7 They searched and searched but they couldn't find the little star. Just then someone tripped over Pooh. "Oww!" he cried. It was Rabbit.

8 "What are you doing down there?" Rabbit asked grumpily. "Looking for a star that just fell out of the sky," explained Pooh.

9 "What? A star's fallen out of the sky!" said Rabbit. "Then we must find it at once!" So Rabbit joined in the search too.

10 Then Rabbit spotted the star, shining on the ground. "There it is!" he shouted, and he bent down to pick it up.

11 "Yeoow!" cried Rabbit. "This star's got a p in it!" "It's my sheriff badge!" smiled Christoph Robin, peering over the bush. "It fell off and I' been looking everywhere for it!"

12 Pooh explained about the star falling out of the sky. "What you saw was a lucky shooting star," said Christopher Robin. "They don't really fall at all." "And we found your badge, so it was very lucky after all," smiled Pooh.

Piglet's drawing page

Can you help Piglet draw the stars
and the moon in the sky? Copy the star
he has drawn. Then, colour in the sky to
make it look dark.

Starry night rhyme

The stars come out at night,
Twinkling in the sky,
Like tiny little diamonds,
Shining from up high.

How many stars can you see?

What do you like about night-time?

● **What colour is Christopher Robin's hat?**

And the shiny, yellow moon,

Looks down on us below,

Brightening up the sky,

With its friendly glow.

● **Is Piglet a Cowboy or an Indian?**

Owl's counting page

How many stars are there?

Are there two or three bats?

Can you see the moon?

12

Owl's family tree

photographs

1 Eeyore wanted to find a new hobby, so he went to ask Owl. "You can help me with my hobby, if you like. I'm making a family tree from these **photographs**," said Owl.

back soon

2 "Look after these," he said, giving Eeyore the box of photographs. "I've got to get something from Christopher Robin, but I'll be **back soon**!"

hello

3 Just then Tigger came bouncing by. "**Hello**, Eeyore. Have you found a hobby yet?" he asked. "Yes," said Eeyore, and he told Tigger all about it.

13

4 "I'm helping Owl make a family tree from these photographs," he said. "**I'll help** too!" said Tigger. "I'll just go and get a spade!"

5 Tigger soon returned with a spade. He dug a big hole in the ground. "**What's that** for?" asked Eeyore. "To plant the box of photographs in," explained Tigger.

6 "**See**, now they'll grow into a family tree," said Tigger, putting the box of photographs in the hole and covering it up. Just then, Owl came back.

14

7 "I've got the card!" Owl declared. "Now we can make a really special family tree!" "We've already done it!" said Tigger, telling him about burying the photographs. "**Oh no!**" groaned Owl.

8 "A family tree is a chart about your family," explained Owl. "I was going to make one by sticking the photographs on this card." "**Sorry**," said Tigger, digging the photographs up again.

9 "Never mind," smiled Owl. "You've given me an idea to make my family tree really special." He put a branch in a pot and hung the photographs on it. "Now I really have got a **family tree**!" he smiled.

Piglet's colouring page

Colour this picture with your crayons. Look at the little picture to see what colours to use.

● What is Tigger doing?

What colour is the spade?

Why is Owl carrying a big piece of card?

How many worms can you see?

17

The raindance

"Are you sitting comfortably, Pooh?" asked Christopher Robin. "Then, I'll tell you a story..."

It didn't rain in The Hundred Acre Wood for a very long time, so Pooh and his friends went to find Christopher Robin. "If it doesn't rain soon, the river will completely dry up," said Pooh, worriedly. "And we'll have no water at all!" "Perhaps if we all try shouting to the clouds, they might let us have some rain!" suggested Christopher Robin. So, they all shouted to the clouds. But nothing happened. "Why don't we do a rain-dance?" said Christopher Robin. "I read all about it in one of my books. Red Indians do them to make it rain." "What a good idea," smiled Piglet. Then, the rain will want to come down and join in the fun." So, they all dressed up as Red Indians and danced around, making

lots of noise. Even Eeyore and Rabbit joined in. It was lots of fun, but soon everyone was feeling a bit tired. "Phew! How long do we have to dance before the rain joins in?" puffed Piglet. "I don't think the rain wants to join in," gasped Pooh. "Why don't you all have a rest for a while?" said Kanga. "I've made everyone a nice picnic to eat while you get your breath back." All that dancing had made them feel hungry, so Pooh and his friends sat down to eat the picnic. Then suddenly the sky went dark and big raindrops started to fall. Plop! Plop! The rain splashed every-where! "Well, the rain didn't want to join in the dancing, but it's certainly come down to join in the picnic," smiled Piglet. They all laughed as they ran inside Christopher Robin's house to finish the picnic indoors!

"Did the river fill up with water again?" asked Pooh. "Oh, yes, which meant there was plenty of water for Rabbit to water his vegetables and for Kanga to do her washing and for Roo to splash about in his paddling pool, too!" said Christopher Robin. "That's good," yawned Pooh. "I'm going to sleep now to dream of picnics and rain. Goodnight." "Goodnight, dear Pooh."

Rabbit's maze

Rabbit can't tell which hose is fixed to the tap. Help him find the right one. Now count how many knots he'll have to untie for it to work.

How many knots are there altogether?

Piglet's drawing page

The river has dried up! Draw some clouds and raindrops, then draw in some water to fill the river up again!

Drought rhyme

The sun's been shining,
For days and days,
Making everything hot,
With its golden rays.

● **How many fishing rods can you see?**

22

The river got so hot,

The water went away,

Now Pooh and Piglet,

Can't go fishing today.

● **What colour is the sun?**

What is Eeyore doing?

Can you find these things in the big picture? Tick the boxes when you see them.

23

On the river

1 Rabbit, Piglet and Pooh had decided to go fishing now that the river was full of water again. "We can use that boat," said Rabbit.

2 So they all got into the boat. "I'll row over to the middle of the river," Rabbit told Piglet and Pooh. "We'll catch more fish there."

3 They were just about to set off when Tigger came along. "Oh, goody, you're going fishing!" he said. "Can I come?" "Of course you can," said Pooh.

4 "I'll go and get my fishing things," said Tigger, bouncing off. "Oh no, Tigger always causes trouble!" groaned Rabbit. "I'm sure he won't this time," said Pooh.

5 "Well, if he doesn't hurry up I'll go without him," said Rabbit. "Here he is!" Piglet shouted a few minutes later, as Tigger came running towards them.

6 "I'm ready!" shouted Tigger. Rabbit stared at all the things he was carrying. "You can't bring all that!" he gasped. "It won't fit in the boat!"

7 "But we need it all," said Tigger, tossing things into the boat. "Look, there's my fishing hat, and a book about fish, and a picnic lunch..."

8 The boat rocked about as Tigger piled his things into it. "Are you sure you need all this?" cried Rabbit. "There are only a few more things," Tigger told him.

9 "See, there's plenty of room," said Tigger. "Oh dear, I hope Tigger doesn't bounce in," said Piglet. "If he does, I think we'll bounce out!" said Pooh.

10 Tigger was just about to get into the boat when he remembered something. "I nearly forgot my fishing rod!" he said, dashing off to get it. "How silly of me!"

11 Tigger soon returned with his rod. "Now we can go," he said. But when he put it on board, the boat got so heavy that it began to sink into the river!

12 "Oops, sorry!" said Tigger as Rabbit, Piglet and Pooh quickly bailed out the water. "Only Tigger could sink a boat without even getting in it!" groaned Rabbit.

Owl's counting page

● **How many fish can you see?**

● **Is there one fishing rod or two?**

● **Can you count the jars of jam?**

28

Piglet's drawing page

Piglet's drawing a picture of himself fishing in the river. Draw his fishing line then join up the dots from 1 to 11 to complete the fish he has caught. Finally, finish colouring the picture.

Pooh's nature notes

Hello, everyone, I'm about to tell you all you need to know about frogs

I'm off!

Frogs have smooth, moist skin, big eyes, long back legs and webbed feet. They move by hopping and leaping. They can swim, too!

● Can you see the frog's long legs?

● Can you hop?

Frogs like to live in damp, grassy places near ponds. They usually hide amongst the grass and plants in the day and look for food at night.

shhhhh!

Can you see the frog hiding in the grass?

dinner!

Frogs like to eat tasty little creatures like slugs, snails and flies. They catch them on their long, sticky tongues, then gobble them up.

Have you ever seen a frog?

Eeyore's door

"Are you sitting comfortably, Pooh?" asked Christopher Robin. "Then, I'll tell you a story..."

Owl popped in to see Eeyore and found him shivering in a corner of his house. "Brr! What a cold day," said Eeyore. "I just can't get warm." "That's because you don't have a door to your house, so the cold comes in," Owl told him. "You're right," said Eeyore. "What I need is a door. But where am I going to get one from?" "We'll make one," said Owl. Owl and Eeyore gathered some twigs and took them back to Eeyore's house.

Then they piled them up to block the doorway. "There!" said Owl. "Now the cold can't get in." "Neither can I!" sighed Eeyore.

they took all the logs and twigs away again. Then they looked for something else to make a door. But they couldn't find anything. "Let's ask Kanga, she might have something we can use to make a door," suggested Owl. Kanga said she thought she had the very thing. She gave Eeyore a thick, white blanket. "Put this over your doorway and it will keep the cold out," she told him. "Thank you," said Eeyore. He hurried home with the blanket. Later, Eeyore's friends decided to visit him and see if he was warm now. But they couldn't find his house anywhere. "It used to be here," said Pooh, puzzled. "But now it's gone." "How strange," frowned Owl. "Oh, dear, Eeyore and his house are lost!" cried Piglet. "Who's lost?" asked Eeyore, peeping out from underneath Kanga's white blanket. He had covered his house with it! "So that's why we couldn't see you!" laughed Pooh. "Your house is white, just like the snow!" "Well, it doesn't feel like snow," said Eeyore, smiling happily. "It's lovely and warm now."

"I'm glad Eeyore wasn't cold any more," said Pooh. "Now I'm going to snuggle down in my nice, warm bed and go to sleep. "Goodnight, Pooh. Sleep tight." "Goodnight, Christopher Robin."

Rabbit's maze

Rabbit wants to go home to get warm. Help him through the maze of scarves and count how many stripes he passe[s]

Tigger's jumper

cold

1 Tigger and Roo were practising their bouncing in Roo's garden. "I'm **cold**," said Tigger. "Me, too," said Roo. "Let's go inside and play." So, they did.

jumper

2 Kanga was in the kitchen, knitting a woolly jumper for Roo. "Ah, there you are, Roo," she said. "Let's see if this **jumper** is long enough yet."

ice

3 Kanga put the jumper against Roo's back. "Hmm, it's still a bit short," she said. "That jumper looks **nice** and warm," said Tigger. "I wish I had one."

35

4 Kanga said she would knit Tigger a jumper as soon as she had finished knitting Roo's. But Tigger didn't want to wait. "I'll kn one myself," he said, getting som knitting needles and wool.

5 So Kanga showed Tigger how to knit. "This is easy!" said Tigger as he started knitting. Roo watched him. "Wow! You're knitting really **fast**!" he gasped.

6 "I'll soon have this jumper finished," grinned Tigger. But ther he ran out of wool. "Where's all the **wool** gone?" he asked, puzzled. "You've wrapped it around yourself!" giggled Roo.

7 "Silly Tigger!" laughed Roo. Kanga and Roo had to untangle him. "I think you'd better **wait** for me to knit you a jumper," Kanga told Tigger.

8 But Tigger had a better idea. He gave Roo one end of a ball of wool and told him to hold it tight. "**Watch** this!" said Tigger, twirling around.

9 Tigger whirled and twirled, winding the wool all around both arms and his body. "Now I've got a nice warm jumper," he said. "That's **clever**!" laughed Roo.

37

Piglet's colouring page

Colour this picture with your pens or crayons. Look at the little picture to see which colours to use.

● What colour is Kanga's wool?

What is happening in the picture?

Have you ever seen someone knit?

How many balls of wool can you see?

39

Hide and seek

1 "I was so looking forward to playing hide and seek today," said Pooh. "But it's raining." "Raining?" said Christopher Robin. "Yes, it's raining leaves," said Pooh.

2 "Silly! The leaves are falling off the trees because it's autumn," Christopher Robin said. "New leaves grow again in the spring." "Oh, good," said Pooh.

3 "We can still play hide and seek," said Christopher Robin. "I'll do the seeking. I'll count to twenty then I'll come and find you." He started to count.

4 Pooh and the others had gone to hide behind the bushes. "18,19,20.... coming!" shouted Christopher Robin. He started looking for his friends.

5 A sudden gust of wind blew the leaves off a bush and Christopher Robin saw Pooh hiding behind it. "Found you, Pooh!" he laughed. "That wasn't a very good hiding place."

6 "He'll never find me behind this big bush," boasted Tigger. But the leaves fluttered from that bush, too. "I can see you, Tigger!" shouted Christopher Robin.

41

7 "And there's Piglet!" he laughed as the leaves flew off the bush Piglet was hiding behind. "Ha, Ha! I've found you all! Now it's Pooh's turn to seek."

8 So Pooh counted to twenty while Christopher Robin, Piglet and Tigger ran to hide. They all hid behind some leafy bushes. "Now where can they be?" thought Pooh.

9 Suddenly, all the leaves fell from those bushes as well! "I can see you all!" shouted Pooh. "This is a waste of time!" grumbled Tigger. "There's nowhere to hide!"

10 Another gust of wind blew a pile of leaves into the air. "The leaves are falling off everything!" said Pooh. "There'll soon be none left."

11 Just then, they realised that Piglet had disappeared! "He must have gone to hide again," said Christopher Robin.

12 Then they heard a cough and a splutter and Piglet scrambled out from a pile of leaves. "The leaves made a good hiding place, after all!" laughed Pooh.

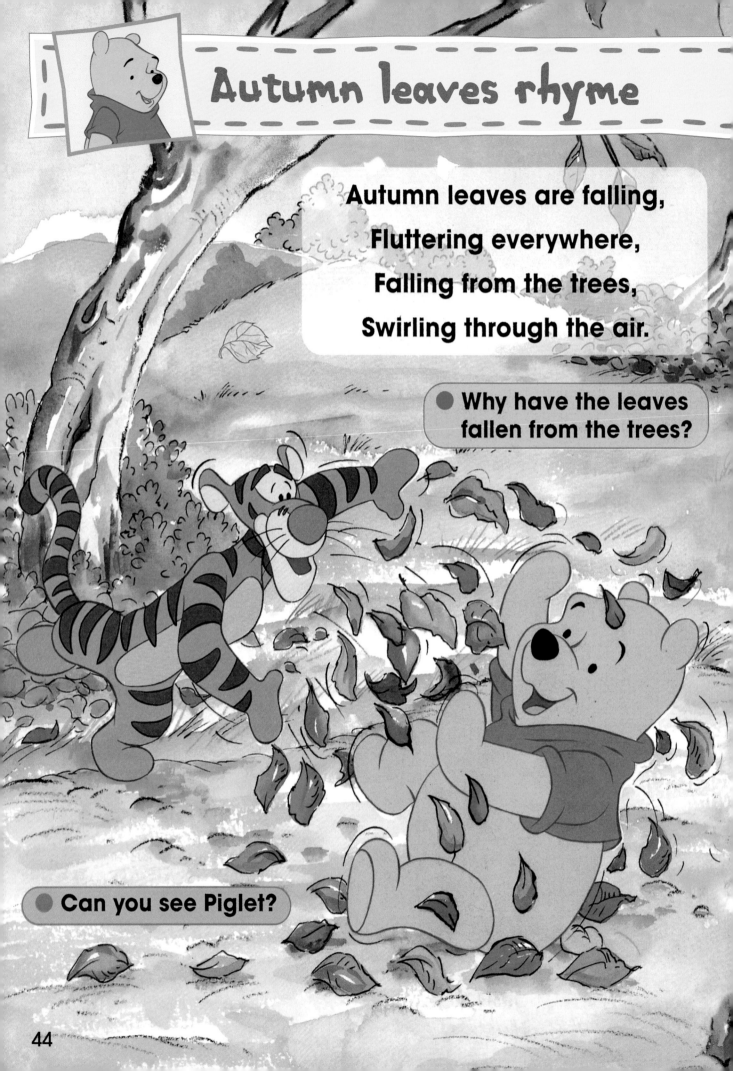

Autumn leaves rhyme

Autumn leaves are falling,
Fluttering everywhere,
Falling from the trees,
Swirling through the air.

● Why have the leaves fallen from the trees?

● Can you see Piglet?

44

Tigger's surprise

Tigger's here to show you how to make some lovely leaf prints. All you need are some leaves, paints, a brush and plain paper.

1 With your brush and paints, paint a leaf your favourite colour.

2 Then press the painted side down onto a sheet of paper.

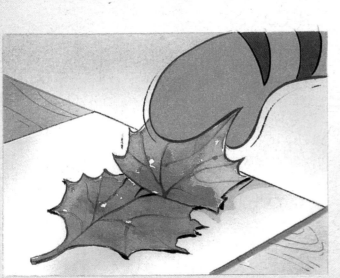

3 Now you have a pretty leaf print. Paint each leaf a different colour and make lots of colourful leaf prints.

Make a Piglet puppet

Here is one of Pooh's friends for you to make into a puppet. All you need are a pair of scissors, some thin card, some paste, some string, four butterfly clips and this page. You might need to ask a grown-up to help.

1 First, stick the pages onto some card. Then carefully cut around the edges.

2 Now put the arms and legs onto Piglet and Roo by pushing a butterfly clip through each hole.

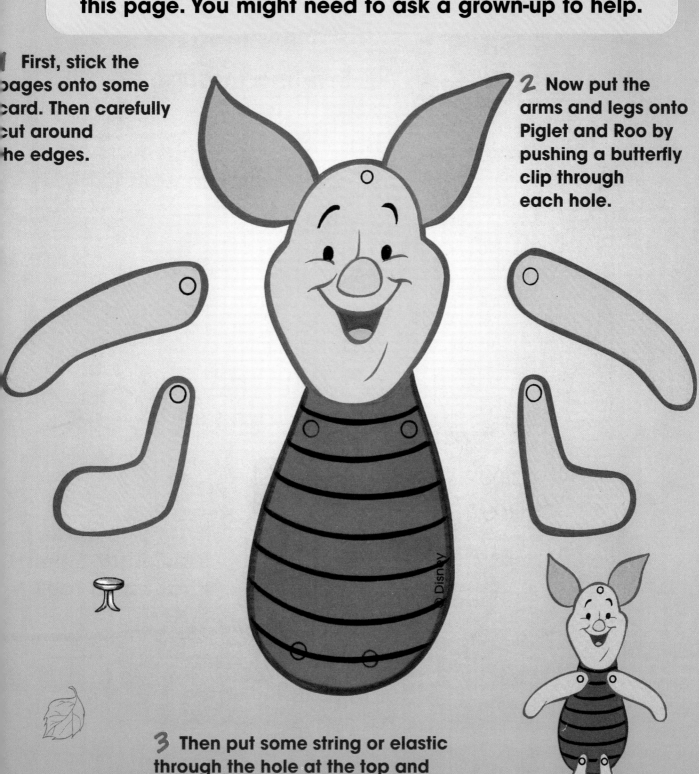

3 Then put some string or elastic through the hole at the top and Piglet and Roo are ready to jump.

Pooh's nature notes

Hello, everyone, I'm about to tell you all you need to know about dormice!

Hello!

Dormice have furry bodies and a long tail. They often make their homes in hedges or at the tops of trees.

● Can you see the dormouse's long tail?

● Can you name any other animal that has a tail?

This **dormouse** is eating some berries from a tree. **Dormice** also like to eat tree flowers and nuts. Their favourite food is hazelnuts.

Yum!

● **How many berries can you see?**

● **What is your favourite food?**

Dormice sleep all day and come out at night. They sleep all winter, too. First, they eat lots of food and then they curl up in their nest and sleep until spring. This is called hibernation.

ZZZzzz,

● **Point to the dormouse's nest.**

The lucky leaf

"Are you sitting comfortably, Pooh?" asked Christopher Robin. "Then, I'll tell you a story..."

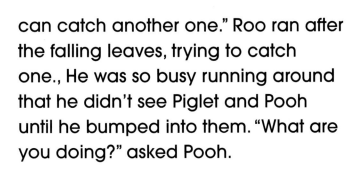

Roo was watching the autumn leaves flutter to the ground as he and Kanga strolled through the wood. "Look at all the different coloured leaves," said Kanga. "Aren't they pretty?" Roo picked one up and put it in his pocket. "I'm going to take one home with me," he said. "It's supposed to be lucky if you catch a leaf before it falls to the ground," Kanga told him. "Do you think you can catch one?" "Of course I can!" said Roo. A leaf fluttered down from a nearby tree and he quickly raced after it. But it fell to the ground before he could reach it. "Never mind," smiled Kanga "See if you can catch another one." Roo ran after the falling leaves, trying to catch one., He was so busy running around that he didn't see Piglet and Pooh until he bumped into them. "What are you doing?" asked Pooh.

I'm trying to catch a leaf before it falls to the ground," explained Roo. "It's supposed to be lucky." "That sounds like fun!" said Pooh, "Let's all try." Roo, Piglet and Pooh all jumped up as a leaf fluttered down and they all bumped into one another! Luckily, Roo managed to grab the leaf just before it touched the ground. "I've got it!" he shouted, holding up the leaf. Piglet and Pooh chased a few more leaves but they didn't catch one.

They were very disappointed. "You can share my lucky leaf," Roo told them. Just then Christopher Robin came along. "Ah, there you are," he said. "I've got a lollipop for everyone." "See, my leaf brought us all luck!" smiled Roo, as they licked their lollipops.

"All that running about has made me feel tired," yawned Pooh. "Counting sheep usually sends me to sleep, I'm sure counting leaves will do the same." "Goodnight then, dear Pooh. Happy counting." "Goodnight, Christopher Robin."

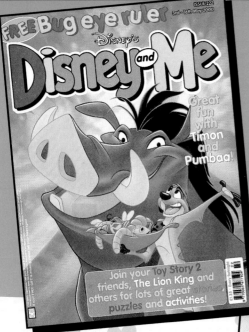

You could win a fantastic family break to

Win!

DISNEYLAND PARIS

Win!

Visitors young and old can discover the magic of Disneyland® Paris with its Theme Park, its seven themed hotels and of course Disney® Village, the entertainment centre.

The Prize: includes two nights bed and breakfast for a family of four at one of the fabulous Disneyland Paris themed hotels*, plus three days unlimited entry into the Disneyland Park.

2001 will be the best year ever at Disneyland Paris!

In addition to over 50 amazing attractions, rides and shows, this year at Disneyland Paris there will be the most fantastic seasonal festivals for you and your family to enjoy!

The year starts off magically at Disneyland Paris, as from January until March 2001 Kids Go Free to the magic. In March you can enjoy all the craic of the Celtic Festival or salsa the night away in the Festival Latino. Summer is always magical at Disneyland Paris and then before you know it... Trick or Treat! Welcome to HalloweenLand! Then, the following month brings the fantastic Bonfire Spectacular Celebrations. Also from November, until the end of the year, it's the magic of a Very Merry Disney® Christmas all wrapped up at Disneyland Paris just for you!

Come and experience the magic in 2001 at Disneyland Paris
Disneyland Paris, The Magic is Closer Than You Think.
For more information on Disneyland Paris call: 08705 030303
or visit: www.disney.co.uk

How to Enter: Unscramble these letters to spell out the name of Mickey's pet dog : LTPOU

Send your answer, along with your name and address to:

Egmont World Ltd,
Deanway Technology Centre,
Wilmslow Road,
Handforth,
Cheshire SK9 3FB.

The closing date for entries is the 12th January 2001.

Snowball throwing

1 Pooh and his friends decided to have a snowball throwing competition. "The one who throws the furthest, wins," said Owl. "**I'll win!**" boasted Tigger.

2 "Huh! I can throw further than you!" scoffed Rabbit. "Are you all **ready**? It's Piglet's turn first," said Owl. So Piglet threw his snowball as far as he could.

3 It landed by a bush. "Very good," praised Owl. "Now it's your turn, Tigger." "Goody!" said Tigger. He made a big snowball. "**Watch** this," he said.

4 Tigger swung his arm around and around really fast. "**There!**" he cried, hurling the snowball through the air. But silly Tigger threw it the wrong way.

5 The snowball went over his shoulder and hit Rabbit on the nose. Splat! Rabbit was very cross. "**Take that!**" he shouted, throwing one back.

6 But Tigger ducked and the snowball hit Pooh! "Ha! Ha! **Missed!**" laughed Tigger. Pooh laughed, too, and threw a snowball at Rabbit, but it hit Piglet instead!

55

7 Soon, everyone was having a super snowball fight. "Right, that's **enough**! Let's get on with the snowball competition!" Owl cried. But no one was listening to him.

8 "**Stop**!" Owl shouted, throwing a big snowball at Tigger. Everyone stared as the snowball whizzed past Tigger, on and on through the air...

9 ...until it hit a big tree and broke. "**Owl's won!**" smiled Pooh. "He threw his snowball the furthest." Everyone cheered. For once, Owl didn't know what to say!

Owl's counting page

- **How many snowballs can you see?**

- **Are there two sledges or three?**

- **Can you count the snowflakes?**

57

Piglet's colouring page

Colour this picture with your crayons. Look at the little picture to see which colours to use.

● **What are Pooh and his friends doing?**

● **What colour is the snow?**

How many snowballs can you count?

Rabbit's maze

Can you help Rabbit through the maze to the finishing post? Count how many snowballs you pick up on the way

Piglet's drawing page

Piglet is drawing a picture of himself and Pooh playing in the snow. Join the dots to see what they are sitting on. Then colour in the picture.